coffee

A Story by
Tom Lang

Also by Tom Lang
eagle
cat
mrs. claus

Published by
BOUDELANG PRESS

Post Office Box 12379
Portland, OR 97212-0379
503.242.0870
Web Site: www.hallucinet.com/boudelang

Illustration and concept by Andrew Reidenbaugh
Design by Siobhan Burns

Library of Congress Catalog Number 95-94650

ISBN 0-9649742-9-0

IF YOU'RE EVER IN JINOTEGA, NICARAGUA, STOP BY
Felipe's and tell him I sent you. No sign, hole
in the wall, middle of nowhere. Some of the
best Jose in the world. Served in a rusty tin
cup. Has that elusive cognac flavor.

Oh yeah, I've drunk coffee all over the
world. I've knocked back many a floral cup of
Ugandan Bugisu in the bullet-riddled coffee
shop at the Entebbe airport. I spent a month

1

one night in a tent 250 miles southwest of Aden drinking bitter, winey (with a hint of cherries) Yemeni coffee out of a fifty-gallon oil drum. My llama and I survived on the gentle acidity of Chanchamayos, the brew that made the Incas famous, while we wandered for weeks, lost but alert, through the Peruvian Andes.

I know about coffee. You bet. I've drunk it all my life. I know about rain. I've lived in Portland, Oregon, all my life. But I don't know much about love, even though I've been in and out of love all my life.

It all started one morning at the Coffee Can in northeast Portland. My hangout. It had been raining steadily, biblically, for months. I'd jumpstarted my day with four or five cups of this nice Malawi blend. Not as refined as Kenyan, but with a hell of a lot more body. I followed that with a couple of lattes while I polished off a two-pound bag of chocolate-covered espresso beans. I tried to read the morning *Oregonian,* but hell, please explain to me how anybody reads that rag. It makes me nervous and sweaty.

I was halfway through my third triple espresso when she walked in the door. She had that caffeinated coffee house look. Dressed in black, of course, and her skin had the pallor of someone raised in a closet. Her eyes, red-streaked road maps, were sunk inside deep, dark, raccoonish circles.

A tiny little bongo player banged triplets on my heart.

Nervous and jittery, she stood in line, the muscles in her face twitching as if this were her first bank robbery. She snapped at an old man with a cane who was slowly placing his order. She picked up her coffee, poured a torrent of sugar, gave the vapors a quick blow, then sucked on the lip of her cup. Her eyes fluttered to a close. Her knees wobbled. She stood in the middle of the cafe, hunched over, clutching her coffee with both hands, a hypothermic wildcatter rescued from the sea.

I stood up. "Over here," I said, spewing sweat out of every pore. "I'm just about to leave."

She stared at me, frowning. I motioned to the empty chair. She nodded. She moved slowly to the table, holding her coffee close to her body, firmly but delicately, an organ to be transplanted. She sat, blew on her cup, swigged like a Viking. Eyes fluttered. Body shook. A post-coital sigh.

She still hadn't spoken. Was she deaf?

4

Mute? I didn't see a problem there. I'd learn to sign. Why not? I was an insomniac anyway. I'd study in the middle of the night when I was usually pacing the floor and pulling out strands of my hair.

I spoke slowly so she could read my lips.

"Those Malawians sure in hell know how to grow a coffee bean, don't they?"

"Yes, the coffees of Kenya and Zimbabwe are too refined and winey for me. Malawi grows as good a bean as anything out of the Kivu or Ituri districts of Zaire."

What a voice, as sweet as a cup of java from the Sigri estate on Papua New Guinea. What guts and intellect to challenge the conventional wisdom on African coffee. Why did I say I had to leave? I had to figure out a way to stay and talk with her. There must be something I could say.

"Do you really have to leave?" she asked.

The mixture of caffeine and love was asphyxiating me. I shook my head. A wheeze of emphysema escaped from a collapsed section of my lungs.

"Good," she said. She pulled a ten-pound tin out of her shoulder bag and placed it on the table.

"Chocolate-covered espresso bean?" she said.

Somewhere a bird sang, a baby cried and the rain stopped.

ARABICA. ARABICA ROBUSTA ROSENAU.

Ironically, she was the great-great granddaughter of Dr. Ludwig Roselius who, in 1908, patented the first process for decaffeinating the coffee bean. He used the French term *sans cafeine* to name his company. Yep. Sanka. But he never saw his dream materialize. He died an old man in 1920 from methylene chloride poisoning, the very chemical that strips caffeine from the bean, turning the manna from the rainforest into the tombstones of the desert.

Sometimes Arabica would grow distant and aloof. I knew she was thinking about her great-great-grandfather, wishing she could have been there so many years ago in Bremen, Germany on the banks of the Weser River. She could have made a difference. Talked some sense into Ludwig. Talked him back into drinking regular coffee. Then, maybe, just maybe, he would be alive today and she would have the great-great-grandfather she never had.

But I get ahead of myself. Arabica and me. We were inseparable. She was new to Portland, and I wanted to show her the Jewel on the Willamette, the city you don't read about in the travel brochures.

I took her to the little greasy spoon on Produce Row that only served Ethiopian, genuine Harrar coffee, made from Longberries, not Shortberries. Our hair and clothes would reek for the rest of the day of the always full-bodied, earthy aroma of cinnamon, fresh-cut grass and rotten strawberries.

We spent many a night at the Cavern, a secret police club in the bowels of the downtown Portland Police Station, drinking buttery Kona Coast brew with Portland's finest. Open twenty-four hours a day, the club had strippers, a firing range and a bakery. It was Portland's worst-kept secret that if you wanted to stay in the coffee business, you kept the boys at the Cavern happy. Fifty-pound sacks of elite beans — "gifts" from the 50,000-odd coffee houses and stores in Portland — were stacked to the ceiling. My seven-year reign as the Coffee

Chugging Champion qualified me for a rare honorary civilian membership.

But we spent much of our courtship behind closed doors. We both loved to cook. Arabica would whip up a dish of fresh coffee pesto. I would bake chicken stuffed with Jamaican Blue Mountain coffee grounds and finished with an espresso glaze. She would poach Chinook salmon in a Haitian Ra-Ra blend, served on a bed of mocha couscous. On a trip to the Oregon coast I prepared my specialty, coffee bouillabaisse, a stewpot of boiling Indonesian Mandheling filled with fresh Dungeness crab, mussels, clams and just a hint of turmeric. On Cinco de Mayo, she made chili with Oaxacan coffee beans and five different peppers. On Fourth of July, I broiled coffee burgers.

And the sex. Yes, the sex. Naked and

blindfolded, we conducted blind taste tests, threatening, in heavily accented voices, the painful consequences of an incorrect identification. For fun, I would mistake the cellary mustiness of Northeast Sumatran for some sludge from Cuba. She would blunder through a tasting, say she "didn't know nothing about coffee," then throw herself at the mercy of the Caffeine Court. We thought of producing an infomercial with local television anchors, sharing our secrets with those in dead-end relationships. Instead, we wrote long, detailed letters to magazines. They, in turn, withheld our name and address by request.

It all came together one night at the Cavern, five months from the day we met. I had just defended my Coffee Chugging title for the eighth time, breaking my old record of eighty-two consecutive cups. While my noble competitors were either vomiting in the corners or in transit to emergency rooms, I gave a humble victory speech.

"...But most of all," I concluded, "I'd like to thank Arabica, without whose support and confidence this would not have been possible. Arabica," I paused, "Will you marry me?"

A silence settled over the crowd. The thuds of my irregular heartbeat echoed off the walls of the club. When Arabica yelled, "Yes! Yes! Yes!" and rushed to my arms, the joint exploded. Confiscated automatic weapons were fired toward the ceiling. Donuts and rolls flew through the air. We sang dirty coffee limericks until dawn.

OUR HONEYMOON WAS WHAT FAIRY TALES ARE MADE of. First stop was the country of the long bluish bean that can be aromatic and acidic, but perfectly balanced with a soft, mild flavor and a heavy body. Guatemala. We ran naked through the plantations of Coban, made love in a roasting room in Huehuetenango, spent a sleepless night, arm-in-arm, drinking iced coffee on the cobblestone streets of Antigua.

Next stop, Managua. We passed on the overrated Matgalpa region, but I showed her the site of the "Battle of the Café con Leche" in the coveted Nuevo Segovia region, considered by many to be the turning point of the Contra-Sandinista War.

I saved Jinotega and the little *tienda* for last. Things had changed, as things do. Felipe still served some of the best brew in the world in those rusty tin cups, but now he sold the cups in sets of four. What once was the outhouse was now a gift shop, stacked full of souvenir T-shirts and baseball caps. There was a six-week waiting list for Felipe's special tour, "Campesino por una dia." For $100, you could work Felipe's shift at the coffee plantation, twelve back-breaking hours in the hot sun with one five-minute siesta to eat the slop the wealthy owners fed the workers. For an extra thirty bucks you could spend the night in one of the vermin-infested shacks and sleep in a real campesino's bunk.

As a wedding present, Felipe offered us a discount (pay for two nights, get the third night free). Moved by his generosity, we hugged and kissed my old friend. "Another time," I told him. I promised that we'd come back for every anniversary.

Before we left, we had Felipe take a photograph of us, snuggled together, just a breath apart, rusty tin cups in hand, arms intertwined, drinking some of the best brew in the world.

In Costa Rica, we toasted our love with gallons of the Dotas of the Terazus region: spicier, more complex and heavier bodied than ever. We decided if there was a coffee shop in heaven, it served Bellavistas from the Tres Rios district — rough yet elegant.

Our last stop was Colombia. The Juan Valdez family had invited us to spend a few days with them. It seems that Juan's grandfather, Juan, knew Arabica's great-great-grandfather from the turn of the century when both were competing for the coffee concession during the building of the Panama Canal. Ludwig lost, but they remained friends, even when Lud drifted into his misguided decaffeinated path.

The patriarch of the family, the once telegenic Juan, had fallen on hard times; he was bedridden and said to babble on about the "ghosts of coffees past, present and future." Some say he never recovered from the death of his son, Juan, gunned down at a coffee tasting in Bogota in 1979, another victim of the bloody coffee cartel wars.

That left the reins to the grandson, Juan, a charming, handsome man who had the highest rated talk show in Colombia. He was enchanted by Arabica and treated us like royalty. We had servants, Uzi-toting bodyguards and a constant flow of Supremo and Excelso Private Reserve. We toured the country in Juan's personal, customized military tank.

It was all like a dream, we said, as we flew home to Portland. Yes, again, like a fairy tale out of an old-fashioned book. Passengers beamed at us. Flight attendants doted on us. We were at the top of the world's waiting list.

By the time we landed at Portland International, we had polished off five pounds of chocolate-covered espresso beans.

"I FEEL YOU TWO HAVE A PROBLEM WITH COFFEE."

Oh, Christ, my brother. Mr. Bandwagon. First it was nicotine and tar, then asbestos, then lead poisoning, then fatty foods and triglyca-whatevers. Mr. Cancer Scare. Mr. Negative.

Okay, granted, this century has seen an accelerated incidence of cancer, but, hey, Mr. Cup-Half-Empty, statistics are for losers.

My brother. What an embarrassment. He was the head of the anti-smoking lobby in the state of Oregon. Can't smoke here, can't smoke there. Secondary this, secondary that. Tax the hell out of it. He led a contingent back to Washington for that Congressional witch-hunt of those railroaded tobacco executives. I wrote a letter to that pretty spokeswoman for the Tobacco Institute and offered her various ways to discredit my brother.

My brother. Now here he was telling me I had a problem. *We* had a problem. I told him, "Yeah, we sure do," and that I knew how to get rid of the problem. Then I slammed the door in his face. No more problem.

Okay, okay, maybe I'm being a little harsh. To my brother's credit, he did bail me out of jail, and — let me back up a bit.

It was a few months after the honeymoon and Arabica and I had slid into a normal rut. Did I say rut? I meant to say routine. Slid into a normal routine. Nothing wrong with that.

We had just finished getting dressed, about to head over to the Coffee Can. We were polishing off our fifth pot of Ethiopian Sidamos and Arabica was filling up our thermos for the walk over. Troubled, Arabica spoke up.

"Honey, is it just me, or does the coffee seem less potent lately?"

"I don't know, maybe," I said, sticking my hands under my armpits in the hope that would stop the shaking.

"It just seems, well... I don't know how to say this."

I felt we were both standing in an earthquake simulator. The clatter of the cup and saucer in her hand evoked the mood of a Mexican hat dance.

"Just say it, dear."

"Well, it just seems that, that —"

"That what?"

"Oh, that we're drinking more and enjoying it less."

Yes, she was right! I knew something was wrong, but I couldn't verbalize it.

Light bulb.

"Yes, Arabica, you're right. And I know why we're drinking more and enjoying it less."

"Why?"

"Because they're diluting the quality of the coffee, blending the good stuff with crap, like Honduran or maybe even decaf."

"Who's doing it?"

"Everybody, probably. The industry. The government."

We nodded sagely, as if we had just solved a riddle of the universe.

We walked down to the Coffee Can, sipping from our thermos.

"I think they've been shorting us on our chocolate-covered espresso beans, too," Arabica said, revelation focusing her thoughts.

"Of course they have," I said.

Our thermos ran dry halfway through the waiting line at the Coffee Can. I began to share our findings with others in line. They shared their epiphanies with us:

"Wow, I thought it was just me."

"So, my dad's right."

"I *thought* I saw black helicopters outside!"

By the time we reached the front of the line, there was a low roar from the hordes behind us.

"Two buckets of Finca San Sebastian," I said to the counter guy, who was swaying his head to the music on the speakers, a compilation of Indonesian pop stars. It sounded like a fleet of fingernails attacking a blackboard.

"Anything else?" he said.

"That used to be more than enough, if you catch my drift," I said.

"Right on," he said, as if I'd just given him a new T-shirt slogan.

I took one swig of my gallon container and slammed it down on the counter.

"This charade is over," I declared.

"Whoa," the counter guy said. The shop went quiet, the only sound the Indonesian music, a dentist's drill with hiccups.

As I told the judge later, it escalated quickly. I don't even remember what I said,

24

though many witnesses described my speech as quite eloquent. One minute I was talking about the integrity and history of coffee, the next minute the counter guy, with his beret, earring and little tuft of hair under his lip, was being dragged over the counter. People were running out the door with espresso machines, aprons, T-shirts, bags of beans, biscotti, muffins.

Afterward, the place looked like a colony of African army ants had marched through. The media, of course, called it a riot. I'll always refer to it as an uprising.

A FEW WEEKS PASSED, REPARATIONS WERE PAID, charges were dropped, my brother's pesterings became a memory.

It was a gala affair — the Portland Police Department's Special Fundraiser at the Cavern. I was to give a coffee-chugging demonstration along with tips on breathing techniques and gullet control. Arabica had volunteered to work the Frisk-for-a-Dollar booth.

Outside of the two mishaps at the chokehold workshop, the evening ran smoothly. I had planned to chug only thirty or forty cups, pose for some photos, and call it a night. But when I chugged the first cup and realized it was Sulawesi, I lost my head. At forty cups, I felt I was catching my rhythm; at fifty, I was in my groove; at sixty, focused; at seventy, driven.

When it dawned on the crowd that I was close to breaking my own record of eighty-three, they began to chant my name. It was the two-minute warning, down by six, eighty yards to go, the cups my wide receivers. I was in the zone. When I grabbed cup number eighty-four, I hesitated briefly, teasing the crowd, then I popped it back, tossing the cup into the chanting cauldron. I heard a bone break, cartilage crunch, a shoulder separate as bodies fought for the memento. I threw my arms into the air, blew kisses with both hands, bowed deeply from the waist. Arabica beamed from her booth while a paramedic frisked her.

Bitten by a subterranean bug, I thought, as the first shot of pain stung my chest. Air vents must be clogged, I thought, as my lungs were sucked dry. Then I felt woozy, feathery, grabbing for a toehold so I wouldn't float away. Then I was falling, collapsing, melting into the ground like a cheap Wizard of Oz stage production.

Fade to black. The last voices I remember:

"Jerry, is it fifteen breaths and two compressions, or fifteen compressions and two breaths?'

"I can never remember."

"Do you have the manual?"

"I left it in the ambulance."

"Wanna go get it?"

"I got it last time."

"TACHYCARDIA. EXTRASYSTOLE. ARRHYTHMIA."

A God-like figure, dressed in white, was standing above me. Other heavenly creatures fluttered nearby. Was this heaven, or was this the waiting area, some type of celestial Ellis Island?

"Tachycardia. Extrasystole. Arrhythmia."

He was talking to me. God was talking to me. Oh, great, I thought, an entrance exam,

31

a spelling bee. Why couldn't it be a sports quiz? Even if I faked my way through the spelling, I'd get nailed in the math section. "An angel leaves Portland with a soul at four o'clock. If there is no time as we know it in the afterlife, when will he arrive in heaven?"

"Hello, I'm Dr. Meili. Listen, all those big words mean this: Our tests show that you have an abnormally fast heart rate, premature beats and some ventricular arrhythmia that, frankly, we've never seen before."

"Is that bad?"

"Well, most of us lost money in the ER pool on whether you were going to make it."

The doctor shuffled some papers. A nurse stopped by and glared at me. The doctor looked up at her.

"Yes, nurse?"

"Oh, nothing, doctor," she said through

clenched teeth. "I just wanted the patient to know how happy I am to see him... *alive*. I was pulling for you." She shot a frozen, gummy smile at me as she walked away.

"We try not to be sore losers around here, but she's been in a diagnostic slump. Happens to the best of us."

He adjusted his glasses.

"Your blood tests are very...ah...interesting. How many cups of coffee did you have yesterday?"

"Let's see... morning... down to the coffee shop... coffee break... afternoon... coffee hour... coffee break... happy coffee hour... chugging contest... Oh, about two hundred cups, I'd guess, give or take twenty cups."

"I'm sorry?"

"I usually only drink half that."

"STOP DRINKING COFFEE?" ARABICA SAID, IN THE SAME tone my mother had used when she had asked my father if JFK had really been shot.

"Just for a little while, honey."

We were standing in the kitchen. I'd just come home from the hospital. We were hugging. She shook in my arms like a five-foot, seven-inch vibrator.

Arabica had outdone herself. I could

smell one of my favorites in the oven — baked ham with a Kenyan Kirinyaga Estate coffee glaze. Espresso mashed potatoes sat on the stove alongside asparagus sauteed in Arabian Mocha. The aroma of Kona peaberry fluttered from our forty-cup coffee dispenser, the size of a beer keg.

"He sounds like a quack," Arabica said. "What do we know about him? Shouldn't we get a second opinion?"

"Honey, it's no big deal. No coffee for a few weeks. How tough can that be? It's not like heroin or something."

We laughed and hugged and kissed.

IT DIDN'T GO WELL.

    When I wasn't looking, during the first leg of my caffeine withdrawal, a tiny, little construction crew crawled up my nose and broke into my cranium. Jackhammers drove shards of skullbone deep into gray matter. Flares and dynamite exploded somewhere near my inner ears. Sheetrock screws were ground into the back of my neck.

Sledgehammers tolled time to the rhythms of my heart.

Actually, all things considered, the first day wasn't bad. The mixture of searing headaches, brain-cell-frying fevers and bone-breaking chills made time fly. The real trouble started when the sun went down.

Arabica was tossing and turning as usual, moaning and screaming through her recurring nightmare of the Decaf Monster. This usually had a calming effect on me, but, for the first time, it didn't seem cute and endearing.

Of course, the bugs didn't help. The worst kind of insects, the kind you can't see, they were crawling everywhere. I finally had to get out of bed, run to the kitchen and spray myself with insecticide. I was just finishing the third aerosol can when I heard the cat.

Fluffy was the neighbor's long-haired something or other. She had fit in my hand as a tiny kitten, purring like a refrigerator. I had played string with her over the years. But as I stood in the kitchen, bugs falling off me in droves, Fluffy's meows cut to my solar plexus like a stiletto. I cursed myself for having been so blind.

For Fluffy was Evil Incarnate. And she must die.

Dressed in black, I stalked Fluffy through the neighborhood. With dental floss wrapped tautly between my fingers, I ached to garrote her and lift the curse she had placed on our home. After three hours of crawling under cars, through bushes and over fences, I went back to the house to reevaluate my strategy.

The night air and the thrill of the hunt

had a mellowing effect on me. After checking for bugs, I slid back into bed, the fatigue of a hard day's work velcroing me to the mattress. It didn't last long.

Lord knows, it wasn't the first time I'd heard the sound, but that night it touched me somewhere vital. Imagine a merengue band using your eardrums for timbales. I was out the door like a fireman, baseball bat in hand. I swiveled my neck and swung the bat to loosen my shoulders while I marched toward the source of the wailing noise. I felt proud and strong and right. When I was done, the car looked like a meteorite that had crashed to earth. In surrender, the alarm belched the last of its bodily functions.

I needed some space. I jumped in my car and drove into the night. I cruised the city in the quiet, early morning hours, fuming at the non-synchronized stop lights, vowing to come back later and shoot them out with my Magnum.

I turned off of Sandy onto Burnside and dipped down toward the bridge. The lights blinded me. I slammed on the brakes, pulled the car to the curb, hit the concrete running. I burst in the door, took a breath, then headed for the counter. The bright yellow and orange decor cheered me up. Something not available in stores droned on the sound system.

"What'll be, honey, a little brake fluid?"

The shoulders of a down lineman, her fingers thick sausages, her hips the width of Montana. I put a twenty on the counter.

"That's right, and keep it coming."

"Refills are free, honey."

It was a commercial blend, probably a

low-grade Brazilian or Colombian, but it was nectar for me. She poured and I drank. And drank. I couldn't drink it fast enough. Coffee was spilling on my clothes, running down the sides of my mouth.

I bought coffee for everyone in the joint. They raised their cups and saluted me. They regaled me with a medley of "Happy Birthday," "Auld Lang Syne" and, I think, a Gregorian chant. I couldn't have asked for a finer group of guys and gals. I promised myself I'd have them all over to the house sometime for coffee lasagna. The transients, the petty criminals, the drug addicts. For that special moment, we were all one. It was four o'clock in the morning and all was well. There would be no more war, hunger, pestilence, if I could just get everybody to sit down with a good cup of coffee. Images of the Nobel peace prize, lecture tours, statues of me in town squares flashed through my mind.

I was giddy. Goofy. I was high. I was cocky and flirtatious. I waved my waitress over.

"Maybe you can settle a little argument I'm having with myself. Now, is this cup of personality I have here in my hand Kenyan Bukoba, or is it Tanzanian Kibo Chagga? I'll be darned if I can tell those two apart."

She raised an eyebrow, shifted her mass, refilled my cup.

"It has that thick, burnt, almost syrupy flavor of Kalosi from the island of Celebes," I rambled on. "But I'd be lying if I didn't admit it also has the slight acidity of Yunnan from south-central China. The Mongols invaded the Yunnan Province in 1253, you know. Stole all their coffee. There are some things you don't do in war, and one of them is you don't plunder a people's coffee. Don't get me started about the Mongols."

I emptied the cup in one fell slurp. I let out an *aaaaah*. The waitress nodded. With the finesse of a blackjack dealer, she poured me another cup.

"Whatever, honey," she said as she walked away.

"It's fiesta time!" I yelled, inspired, jumping up from my stool. Startled, a skinny teenager, dressed in tent-sized clothing, dropped his tube of glue. A hooker shoved her syringe into her purse. A man in the corner quit barking at the wall.

I taught my new amigos and amigas the Cumbia Coffee Dance, an homage to the Coffee God I'd learned one summer while working on a coffee ranch in the Bucaramanga region of Colombia. With coffee cups balanced on our heads, we line-danced through the all-night diner, out into the street, across the Burnside Bridge, back over the Steele Bridge and into our seats. This is what life was all about, I said to myself. Why couldn't every night be like tonight, I wished. I glowed with the human warmth from my simpatico friends.

I took the coffee cup off my head, sat down at my stool and watched my waitress pick up a fresh pot from the coffee maker. She walked over to me.

"You can sure put it away, honey," she said as she poured, the flowing coffee caressing my cup.

I looked at my watch. Where does the time go, I thought? It was dawn and I had to get home. Arabica would be worried. I stood up, caffeine pulsing through my body like spinach. I hugged the waitress as well as physically possible, kissed her full on the lips and told her if I wasn't married I'd take her away from all of this. She smiled the smile of someone who'd heard it a million times.

As I turned to go my mouth began to water, sweat drenched my face. My stomach churned and sputtered like an antique automobile. I spun around, dazed, looking for privacy. I rushed out the door, fell down at the curb and began to vomit in the gutter. My new-found friends came out of the diner and surrounded me as I heaved on the corner. My pocket was gently picked. My watch was stripped from my wrist. Someone wrestled with my shoes.

I finally stood up, dug my car keys out of my pocket, wiped off my mouth with my sleeve. The waitress walked over and yanked the keys out of my hand.

"You're in no condition to drive," she said. "Let me call you a taxi."

She helped me into the cab and stuck a piece of paper in my pocket.

"I think you've got a problem with coffee, honey. Call me if you feel like it."

Arabica was on the porch in her robe and slippers, her cup and saucer tap-dancing in her hand. The police were restraining my neighbor, who was showing the officers a magazine ad of what his car used to look like. As I walked up the steps, Fluffy hissed at me.

A rookie cop stared at me until recognition kicked in.

"Hey, wow, you're the coffee-chugging champion, aren't you?"

"Not anymore," I said.

"ARE THERE ANY CAFFEINE ADDICTS HERE TONIGHT?"

Yeah, yeah, that's me, yoo-hoo, over here. I was powerless over coffee. I admit it. At least I admit it here in this old church. Tell my brother and I'll deny it like a senator.

I didn't have a problem with the basic tenets of Caffeine Anonymous, but some of the policies irked me. I understood, of course, not serving caffeinated drinks, but no smoking and no cookies? With the help of my waitress at the late-night diner, I found a renegade meeting. You could smoke and eat doughnuts, and everybody used their last names instead of that stupid first-names-only crap. They even served beer and shots of tequila at the break.

"This here contains tannic acid."

The speaker was at the podium, holding a coffee bean between his fingers. An Ethiopian Harrar. Longberry.

"They use tannic acid to tan leather. That's right, animal hides. Do you feel that your regular cleanser isn't getting those tough grease spots out of your stove, kitchen floors, counter tops? Coffee will. One of the most abrasive cleaners known to man. Gee, I wonder what it does when we drink it?"

Ooohs and aaaahs, groans, gagging sounds from the multitude. The speaker continued.

"I'd drink fifteen, twenty cups of coffee. IN ONE DAY!"

Whistles. Whoas. Whews.

"I'd eat a five-pound can of chocolate-covered espresso beans. EVERY WEEK!"

A shaking of heads, a communal exhalation of breath.

I slumped in my chair, a serial killer thrown in with library card violators.

IT WASN'T EASY KICKING CAFFEINE, BUT THE meetings helped. My sponsor was great. He belonged to sixty-seven different twelve-step programs, from Lawyer Novels Anonymous, to a program for people who were powerless over using "you know" in their speech. But the home life was another story.

A large part of love is being able to share your daily experiences with your partner. I would come home from a meeting, brewing over with information. I would tell Arabica about the central cortex, which handles thought processes, and the medulla, which regulates heart rate, respiration and muscular coordination, and how caffeine stimulates these sections of our brain, causing that hyper, jittery feeling that caffeine addicts know so well.

I would draw diagrams on our kitchen message board, showing how caffeine relaxes the muscles in the respiratory system, the digestive tract and the kidneys, causing increased urination.

While I was sketching the locus ceruleus, the nerve center near the top of the spinal cord that is involved with the control of our heart rate and respiration, I looked at Arabica. She was slumped over in her chair, her head in her hands. I rushed to her.

"I'm sorry, honey," I said. "I know this is quite a bit to absorb. I'll save neuromodulators and Restless Leg Syndrome for tomorrow."

She was crying, sobbing.

"Is something wrong?" I asked.

"Everything's wrong," she cried. "I don't know you anymore. We don't talk anymore. You just talk at me. And now you sleep all night. Who am I supposed to talk to in the middle of the night while I pace the floors?"

"We could have a baby, honey."

"That won't solve anything."

"You're probably right," I said, "considering the possible link of caffeine with an increased incidence of breech deliveries, infants with low birth weight, stillbirths, miscarriages and premature births."

"I see where this is going!" Arabica yelled, standing up and spilling her coffee on the floor. The Mexican blend, with its hint of hazelnuts, tickled my nose. "Next thing you're going to say is I have a problem with coffee."

Arabica reached for the coffee pot for a refill, but found it empty. She shook it savagely, opened the top and searched inside as if there were a secret coffee compartment, then slammed it to the floor. She was making the quick, jerky movements of a short-circuited robot.

"I'm going to pretend I didn't hear that," she said.

"I didn't say anything, Arabica."

"Hah!" she said as she stumbled her way out of the kitchen and slammed the bedroom door.

I slept on the couch.

I NEVER SAW HER AGAIN. I WENT TO A MEETING the next morning, came back with flowers, but she was gone. Took everything that tied us together. The collection of antique percolators, the coffee vacuum, the French press, the drip, the French drip, the Neapolitan flip, the espresso machine, the roaster, the recipes.

She left a note. Sort of. It was all wet with the ink smeared when I found it. I could decipher a couple loves, two needs and a want.

Oh, she left the photo on the wall over the kitchen table where we drank coffee every morning. It's a picture of us at Felipe's outside of Jinotega. Rusty tin cups in hand, arms intertwined, we're drinking some of the best brew in the world. When I'm sitting there alone, I can taste that elusive cognac flavor

I've become a pillar at the old Caffeine Anonymous meeting, but again, don't tell my brother. I told him I joined a cult that worships nicotine, asbestos and lead.

I've even gotten to like those half-brewed pseudo-addicts. And they listen to reason. I insisted, because of my record-setting coffee consumption, that I receive triple bonus chips for every day I'm java free. They finally came around.

But don't think I'm getting soft. A new-comer came to a meeting the other night saying he was powerless over decaf. I drop-kicked his butt right down the church stairs. I also eliminated two of the steps I always thought were stupid, so now we're the only ten-step program in town.

But between you and me, I sit at that kitchen table way too long and I think about Arabica way too much. I know I am living life more, but damn, I'm enjoying it less.

BOUDELANG PRESS ORDER FORM

Name_____

Street_____

City_____State_____Zip_____

Add $1 for shipping on individual book orders. For 3 or more books, add a flat $3.

Please send the following:

	mrs. claus			TOTAL
Quantity	_____			x $7 = _____
	coffee	cat	eagle	
Quantity	_____	____	_____	x $5 = _____

Shipping   + _____

                                    TOTAL DUE = _____

Please make checks payable to : BOUDELANG PRESS
                                                  P.O. BOX 12379
                                                  Portland, OR 97212-0379

Questions? Please call: 503.242.0870

New! Order directly from our website,
www.hallucinet.com/boudelang